I dedicate this book to my parents, for carrying me as their seed
and growing me with love.
To my children, for being my seeds, whom I cultivate with
infinite, pure love.
To my husband, for being our sun and helping all of us flourish.
To all the children of the world, wishing that they grow
healthy and majestic like the trees.
A special "thank you" to my friend and photographer, Vivi Bohrer
(vivibohrer.com) for my biography picture, and to my cousin,
professional interpreter and translator, Tais Leal de Oliveira
(tais.leal.de.oliveira@gmail.com), to Tom Blodget and Char Prieto
for their input. Gratitude!
To my family and friends for being part of my journey on this
beautiful and generous earth.

Thank you,

– Aline de Oliveira Green

02/21

To the Meilandt family, with TONS of love,

Aline Green

The Seed: Beauty in the Life Cycle of a Maple Tree (1st Edition 2018)

Written by Aline Green. Illustrated by Kate Zotova. Edited by Shari Schwarz. Copyright © 2018 Aline de Oliveira Green. All rights reserved.

Written by Aline de Oliveira Green

Illustrated by Kate Zotova

THE SEED

BEAUTY IN THE LIFE CYCLE
OF A MAPLE TREE

It was a beautiful, windy day in October. The sun was shining, and the birds were singing. The trees were tall and majestic.

2

Then, a strong gust of wind blew.
The branches of the trees shook so hard
it looked like they were dancing.

3

4

5

Leaves, pine cones, pine needles and seeds were flying around. A cute one swirled to the ground, right onto the dirt.

What does it look like to you? It's a helicopter seed! They come from maple trees. (Did you know that maple syrup comes from the sugar maple tree?).

Following the wind storm came the rain,
soaking the earth and burying the little seed.
It was dark all around, and the seed felt cold.

After many days of rain, the clouds finally dissipated. The sun shone bright, warming the ground. Soon enough, the seed tried to reach out for the sunshine.

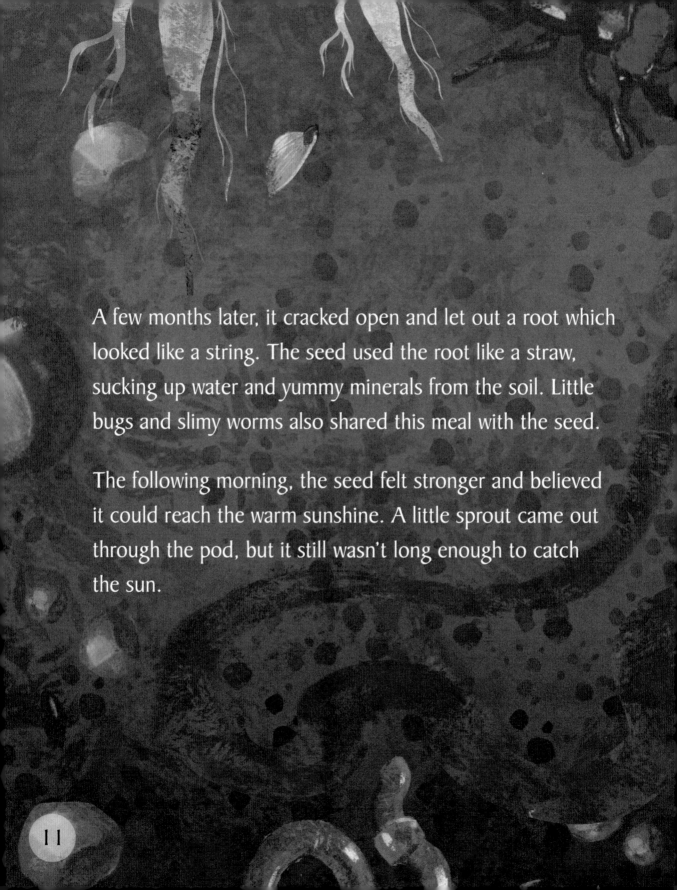

A few months later, it cracked open and let out a root which looked like a string. The seed used the root like a straw, sucking up water and yummy minerals from the soil. Little bugs and slimy worms also shared this meal with the seed.

The following morning, the seed felt stronger and believed it could reach the warm sunshine. A little sprout came out through the pod, but it still wasn't long enough to catch the sun.

The seed kept drinking from the rain and eating from the earth. The sprout grew longer, and it even had a couple of leaves on the tip! It made an extra effort to stretch out, and it felt so good to finally feel the warmth of the sun.

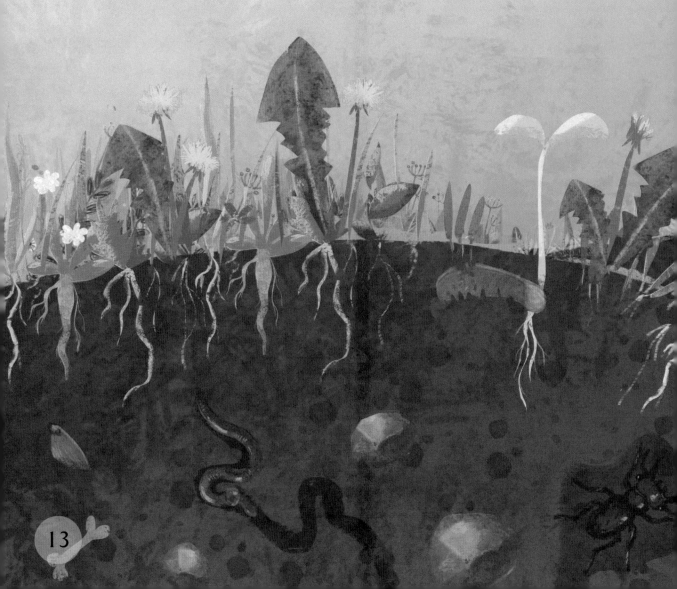

Years went by and all that healthy eating and drinking turned the seed into a beautiful and happy TREE!

14

Every morning, the tree felt the sun's warmth and grew even closer to the big star. (Did you know that the sun is a star?) Every time it rained, the tree drank more water and got refreshed.

The wind blew through its branches making them dance, and the leaves smiled at the sun.

16

Squirrels, birds, ants and other bugs
lived in the tree throughout the seasons.

Many years later, the once little
helicopter seed realized it was now a tall
and majestic tree, with long branches,
a strong trunk, bright green leaves
and…new little seeds! It felt so happy!

SPRING

SUMMER

FALL

WINTER

18

Then, on a beautiful, windy day in
October, a strong gust of wind blew…
and started the cycle all over again.

19

Aline de Oliveira Green is from Rio de Janeiro and currently lives in California with her husband, two children and their dog. They're all bilingual, even the dog! She has a bachelor's degree in Journalism and specialization in Portuguese and foreign language teaching methodology. After working as an English and Portuguese teacher for a while, Aline moved on to become a life coach and author. Her mission is to educate and coach using her skills and also help fellow humans add more joy to their lives.

Dear Reader: What did you think of this story?
Please give your opinion and remember to rate this book on Amazon's website. It is very important to me and other readers! Thank you.

www.aline.green

Made in the USA
Middletown, DE
04 January 2021

29686609R00015